Dear Parents:

Congratulations! Your child is taking the first steps on an exciting journey. The destination? Independent reading!

STEP INTO READING® will help your child get there. The program offers five steps to reading success. Each step includes fun stories and colorful art or photographs. In addition to original fiction and books with favorite characters, there are Step into Reading Non-Fiction Readers, Phonics Readers and Boxed Sets, Sticker Readers, and Comic Readers—a complete literacy program with something to interest every child.

Learning to Read, Step by Step!

Ready to Read Preschool–Kindergarten
• big type and easy words • rhyme and rhythm • picture clues
For children who know the alphabet and are eager to begin reading.

Reading with Help Preschool–Grade 1
• basic vocabulary • short sentences • simple stories
For children who recognize familiar words and sound out new words with help.

Reading on Your Own Grades 1–3
• engaging characters • easy-to-follow plots • popular topics
For children who are ready to read on their own.

Reading Paragraphs Grades 2–3
• challenging vocabulary • short paragraphs • exciting stories
For newly independent readers who read simple sentences with confidence.

Ready for Chapters Grades 2–4
• chapters • longer paragraphs • full-color art
For children who want to take the plunge into chapter books but still like colorful pictures.

STEP INTO READING® is designed to give every child a successful reading experience. The grade levels are only guides; children will progress through the steps at their own speed, developing confidence in their reading.

Remember, a lifetime love of reading starts with a single step!

DreamWorks Trolls © 2023 DreamWorks Animation LLC. All Rights Reserved. Published in the United States by Random House Children's Books, a division of Penguin Random House LLC, 1745 Broadway, New York, NY 10019, and in Canada by Penguin Random House Canada Limited, Toronto.

Step into Reading, Random House, and the Random House colophon are registered trademarks of Penguin Random House LLC.

Visit us on the Web!
rhcbooks.com

Educators and librarians, for a variety of teaching tools, visit us at RHTeachersLibrarians.com

ISBN 978-0-593-70279-6 (trade) — ISBN 978-0-593-70280-2 (lib. bdg.)
ISBN 978-0-593-70281-9 (ebook)

Printed in the United States of America

10 9 8 7 6 5 4 3 2 1

DREAMWORKS

Band Together

FAMILY HARMONY

by Mei Nakamura

Random House 🏠 New York

There once was a boy band
named BroZone
that everyone loved.
It was made up of
five brothers.

The youngest member
was Baby Branch.
But one day, the
band broke up.

Grown-up Branch

still likes to sing.

But he likes to hang out
with his friend Poppy
best of all.

Poppy is the leader
of the Pop Trolls.

She is happy
and full of energy.
She loves to sing,
dance, and hug!

Poppy finds out
Viva is her sister.
They are so happy!
They dance, hug,
and sing together.

Viva is the leader of
the Putt-Putt Trolls.
She lives on an old
mini-golf course.
Viva always
protects her tribe.

Velvet and Veneer
are famous pop singers.
Fans adore them!
But they have a secret.

Velvet and Veneer
stole Troll talent
to become great singers.

Crimp is Velvet
and Veneer's helper.
She always tries
to work hard.
But Velvet and Veneer
are so demanding!

Floyd is one of
Branch's older brothers.
Velvet and Veneer captured
him for his Troll talent!

John Dory is

Branch's oldest brother.

He was the leader of BroZone.

John Dory needs his brothers

to help save Floyd!

Spruce is Branch's
second-oldest brother.
He lives on Vacay Island.
He likes to chill.

Clay is the middle brother.
He lives with the
Putt-Putt Trolls.
Clay is Viva's
right-hand man.
He is serious—but has
a silly side, too!

This is Tiny Diamond.

He does not want

to be treated like a baby.

Tiny Diamond helps

Branch and Poppy find Floyd.

Gristle and Bridget
are king and queen
of the Bergens.
Bergens are so big!

Bridget and Poppy
are best friends.
They do not need to be
related to be like sisters.

Branch and his brothers
find and save Floyd!
They sing in harmony.
They also get the band
back together.

Poppy and Viva
lend their voices
to BroZone.
Everyone cheers!

Poppy is so happy

that she and Branch

have found their families!